Lost Tales

Nobility, deception, love and jealousy

SJ Ball

✳

Published by SJ Ball

First published in Great Britain in 2016
by SJ Ball

I

Copyright © SJ Ball 2016

The right of SJ Ball to be identified as the Author
of the Work has been asserted by her in
accordance with the Copyright, Designs and
Patents Act 1988.

ISBN 978-0-9954508-0-6

To J and S

With all my love

Lost Tales

 England's rains don't care at all
About whose heads they choose to fall,
Upon a stately Royal brow,
A licey head or dirty cowl,
It drives its victims to seek shelter
Against its merry helter skelter.
And so now comes a King and fellows
Soaking, as the Gateman bellows,
"Hold your horses, hold your tempers
Locks like these won't stand for meddlers,
Let me get the bolts shot proud
And then we'll see who shouts so loud."
His face was quite a different pallor
From its red and beery colour
When he saw who stood without.
"Fetch the Guard and Lord!" he shouts,
"Come in my Liege" he says while squirming,
Scratching at his backside vermin,
"Come in, forgive my poor mistake
Of who it was here at my gate."
He tries to help the King dismount
And from a courtier gets a clout

And seeing all the others laugh
Runs off to tell the Castle staff.
The Castle Lord, Sir Robert Smee
Bows and goes upon his knee,
"Enter please my poor abode
You do me honour noble Lord."
Now imagine all the mutter,
All the rushing and the flutter,
Wine and beer and honeyed mead,
Food prepared at double speed.
At last the King said he'd retire
And went accompanied by his Squire
And gradually all went their way,
To lay amongst the dogs and hay.
But soon the storm grew even louder,
Raging round the castle tower,
Fires blew out and candles simpered,
Door jams whistled, children whimpered,
Then the thunder came and roared
And sleet and rain grew more and poured
Until at last in desperation
The King called out "To great damnation!
To sleep through this one must be dead.
Help me get out of this bed!
Since the gods make so much din,
I must go seek the noise of men."

He snatched his gown and stormed off out,
Kicking at the drowsy louts
Who lay about the castle floor,
"Get me mead!" they heard him roar.
Soon the castle all assembled
In the main hall, quite dishevelled,
Round the fire they stood and sat.
"Now tell us Smee, what are we at?"
The King demanded of the Lord
"A night like this should be ignored.
Entertainment we require,
What's on offer? Where's my Squire?"
The Squire came running to his side
"Now use your brains boy and decide
What amusement we can seek
To pass a night that seems a week."
The Squire screwed his pallid brow
And scratched his ear and then said "How
About a tale from thee and me
And all this noble company?
I have no doubt assembled here
Are tales enough to last a year."
"Clever lad, an inspiration!"
Said the King, while consternation
Spread around the gathered folk,
Who would be the first to talk?

✳

Now in the corner stood a fellow
In whose ear a ring of yellow
Glittered in the torches light,
He looked a rum one for a fight.
All his clothes were dull and leather,
Hardened from the bitter weather
And his smile? As cold as ice,
You could tell nothing from his eyes.
A Captain of the sea and foam
"Come Sir, you are far from home"
The King called while the man turned paler,
"I see you are a hardened sailor.
Surely there's a tale or two
To be told by the likes of you?"
The man came forward bowing low,
"Goodly King, though few I know
There is one tale I'd like to tell
If your Liege will wish me well?"
"The man's a sport!" the King declared,
"Tell your tale sir, don't be scared,
A bit of smut or something rude
Would do us all a lot of good."
So sitting down and gulping ale,
The Captain coughed and told his tale.

The Sea Captain's Tale

 A Captain of the sea had docked
In his ship 'The Golden Lock'
To take on board his goods and then
To straight away set sail again.
He had no time for gay disport
Among the taverns of the port.
Anxious then to get away
He pushed his men throughout the day.
And only when all was stored tight,
Did he dismiss them for the night.
"Be back early" then he warned
"For we set sail at light of dawn."
After eating he retired
But seldom had his night attire
On about his brawny person
When a knock caused him to curse and
Throwing wide his cabin door
He saw a woman stood before.
She had quite a comely face
And dressed in velvet and in lace
It seemed to him she was not short
For money, jewels and all that sort.

Now this Captain was a crafty fellow
And so, pretending to be mellow
Bowed to her and said "My dear,
Whatever are you doing here?
Did you not know that ships at night
Are not the place for ladies. Right
Away turn round and leave my craft"
(As I said he was not daft).
She responded as he'd hoped
"Noble Captain, Sir" she spoke
"I ask for passage on your ship
I'll pay and even work for it.
Do not turn me from your door,
As you see I am not poor,
But I must leave here by tomorrow,
My poor heart is full of sorrow!
Take me with you, just to Spain,
And ease a lady of her pain."
Of course he said, "Now, now, there, there,
Come and sit down in my chair"
And like the craft dog he was,
Soon heard all her tale of woes.
I need not trouble you with them,
Suffice to say it concerned men.
And soon affairs were all agreed,
Next day she joined him out to sea.

This salty Captain was the sort,
Who normally disliked to sport
And merely had financial gain
Imprinted soundly on his brain.
But as the days went swiftly by
And as at night he heard her sigh
From the cabin next to him
His thoughts turned slowly round to sin.
And so one day the Captain said
"Tonight my dear when you're abed,
You must do just as I say,
For we pass over Neptune's grave
And at the midnight hour will he
Rise with Trident from the sea
And if you wish to see the day
There are some rules you must obey.
Lay quite naked on your bed
And do whatever Neptune says.
For he expects a toll you see
For safe passage on his sea."
She thanked the Captain from her heart
For his advice and lay quite stark
And naked on her bed that night
And sure enough, at twelve a mighty
Knocking sounded on her door.

"It is Neptune, hear him roar!"
She whispered to herself and lay
As Neptune entered and did say
"A fare, a toll, you owe to me
For passing o'er my treacherous sea!"
"Neptune" then the woman cried,
"Take your toll from such as I,
I am but of mortal sod,
I would not deny a God."
So doffing off his soaking gown
And seaweed from his hair and crown,
Neptune did extract his fare
And what goings-on were there.
For in the half light she was blind
To Neptune's form, a mortal kind,
And when he took his leave she sighed
And slept, while next door, very tired
The Captain hid his God's apparel
And slept as well, the naughty fellow!
In the morning he enquired
As to why she looked so tired
And she told him that she'd done
What he said, and thanked him some
For teaching her the sea's old lore
"But Madam, I regret there's more!"
The Captain cried and said to her

"Poseidon too requires his fare.
Tomorrow morn we dock in Spain
But if you wish to live – again
You must do as you did last night.
I am so sorry for your plight."
And so when the evening came,
On her bed she lay again,
Trembling in anticipation
Of the Sea Lord's reputation,
While next door our fair Poseidon,
Garbed in seaweed, but no Trident,
Readied himself at her door
And then burst in with mighty roar.
Said "Where's the maiden that I hear
Paid my brother Neptune's fare?"
The rest I leave you to imagine
All that happened in that cabin,
Until at last the sun arose
And land was sighted very close,
While at the helm the Captain smiled,
Looking just a little tired.
They docked and loaded off and then
The Lady with her luggage came
And happily she bid adieu
To the Captain and his crew.
She thanked him for a pleasant trip,

For his good advice and tips
And said that when she should leave Spain,
Could she sail with him again?
The Captain told her certainly,
And thanked her for her generous fee.
She left and never realised
She'd paid not once, or twice, but thrice!"

The King sat laughing for a while
And then said "Sir, I like your style,
That Captain was a clever dog,
I note you don't say who he was
And I won't ask, but now I fear
Your business will increase this year!
That tale will be on many a lip,
Watch out for women on your ship!
And now I think a lady must
Respond to this bold tale of lust.
Who will be the woman then,
To tell a tale of foolish men?

A voice then spoke behind the King,
Rich and deep, a sensuous thing.
"I have a tale to please your Lord

If leave you'll grant me to hold forth?"
"Madam, please" the King called out,
"Reveal yourself, now come about"
And from the corner of the crowd,
Came a woman tall and proud,
Full breasted, middle aged and fine,
With laughing eyes and lips like wine.
Dressed in cloth of warmest hue,
"Now Madam, tell us who are you?"
The King enquired leaning back,
(There was no much this lady lacked).
At which point up jumped Robert Smee,
Bowed and went down on his knee,
"Allow me to present my wife,
Who is the treasure of my life"
While glancing at the startled King.
"Well Smee, what a wondrous thing!
Who would think upon these moors
Behind your bleak forbidding doors
Dwelt a lady quite so fine.
I wish your secret could be mine!"
Smee laughed out loud and said "My dear,
Tell the King how you are here
And assure him I possess
No great secret or prowess."
So turning to the King she said

"My Lord, Sir Robert and I wed
Only just the other week.
He took me from a life so bleak
And brought me here to live and rest,
He gave me more than just the best.
I was once a courtesan
And I knew how to please a man,
But flowers fade and trees grow old
And so I withered and was told
By the man with whom I stayed
Someone else was in my place.
So out into the street I went
And as I could not pay the rent
Or buy the things my trade required
I feared that soon I would expire,
So worked in laundries and in inns,
Becoming old and very thin,
Unwanted then, not as before
When suitors queued up at my door.
Until one evening leaving work
I fell down face first in the dirt,
And who should pick me up but he
Who later made me Lady Smee.
He was kind and gentle and
Was quite unlike the usual man.
He made me what I am today

And never asked that I should pay
In any way for what he'd done,
He is a great man Sire, for none
Can know him the way I do.
I recommend him much to you."
By this time the poor old Knight
Had gone quite red and muttered "Right
My dear, no more I pray,
Tell us what you have to say."
"Not so fast!" the King replied,
"Smee, though you are old and tired
And scarred by life I see your heart
From many others stands apart
As an example to all here
Of how a Knight should thus appear.
Kind and gentle, knightly Smee,
You shame us all, including me
But I can see your comely wife
Appreciates her Lord and life.
If we all but did as you do,
We should all be blessed as you.
Now Madam, sit you down and speak
Upon how man is dim and weak,
Apart of course I must now add
From your husband, lucky lad!"
And so the Lady settled down,

Arranged her hair and hands and gown
And cleared her throat and said "A Tale
To shame the most stalwart of males!"

Lady Smee's Tale

The capitals of cities give
A man a chance to really live.
Girls and gambling, secret inns,
Crime and passion, all the sins
Can be found within their walls,
A man need not look hard at all
To sample all the fine delights
Of crime and love and duels and fights.
Now once to one such city came
A man who bore a famous name
And in amongst his retinue
He brought his page and Squire too.
The page does not concern us here,
It is the Squire who will appear
Foremost in this tale of mine.
He was young and very fine
And conscious of his beauteous face,
So dressed himself in finest lace
And silks from northern Italy.
He would not appeal to me
But pandered to his Master's whim,
Who duly tolerated him.

This master was a rogue, and clever,
Making sure he never ever
Got caught out while at his game
And so he kept his famous name.
He played the field of noble wives
Left alone by men whose lives
At Court kept them away by day.
Upon their loneliness he played,
His main ambition being bed,
He'd sampled many it was said.
But yet he equally adored
To stand there at a lady's door
And woo her with his fiery eyes,
His sneaky smile and phoney sighs,
He felt it sporting and a game,
To win is nice but not the same
As if you have to fight a bit,
And he was very good at it!
And so perchance one night he said
To his Squire, just before bed,
"There is a lady I have seen,
A creature quite divine. I've been
By her house in Lambrey Street,
Very soon I hope to meet
Her. After that, well, we shall see,
I think she may fall prey to me!"

Engrossed then with this jolly thought,
He did not see how tense and fraught
His Squire looked as he retired,
Nor realized the plan inspired
In the young man's simple mind,
By his boasts of womankind.
Jealously is not a seed
One should not tend to or heed,
For sown unnoticed it will grow
To great proportions and if so
Can cause great problems unforeseen
And so the Squire began to scheme.
Why should he just merely serve
When higher things he did deserve?
His master, classy but a bore,
A face like his could do much more.
And so this vain and silly boy
Set out next day upon a ploy
To equal him in other's eyes
With the Master he despised.
To the house in Lambrey Street
He trotted on his pretty feet
And boldly knocked upon the door
When, waiting for an answer saw
Behind a curtain such a face!
At least his master had good taste

And for a change he would be first
To take the plunge and quench his thirst.
All these thoughts in him were fired
And strengthened by a great desire,
So that when the door was opened
And the maid enquired who called, then
In his best voice he demanded
"Let me pass unreprimanded!
'Tis your mistress that I seek,
She and I have need to speak."
He gave the maid his master's name,
(For he was posing as the same)
And dressed in lace and all that lark
Once could say he looked the part.
So thinking him a noble man
The maid said "wait" and off she ran
To her lady's room and asked
If the man below should pass
And would her ladyship receive
A man who, without prior leave,
Had sought to push in past her door.
The lady said "Bring him before
Me, for though I don't know his face,
His reputation in this place
Has overtaken him so fast,
I'm glad I was not left till last!"

And so the Squire was shown in
And straight away he did begin
To charm and flatter and to woo
With all his might this woman who
Must have been quite twelve years older,
Undeterred he got still bolder
By asking could he call again?
Relying on his master's name
To open up this lady's door
Once more for him, as before.
The Lady thought, and then said "yes
Come again in two days hence"
And so he left her thinking he
Next time surely would achieve
That which all men have in mind
And so he went home satisfied.
When he'd left the lady called
Her maid and said "Now I am told
That the man he claimed to be
Was big and dark, older than me,
Not a vain and pretty youth,
Now I intend to find the truth!
Find out where the Lord resides
And bid him hasten to my side.
Tell him that I quite forgot
To tell him something and I'll not

Go to bed 'til he is here,
Hurry now, don't fail my dear."
And so the maid found out the home
Of the master and was shown
By a servant for some gold
To his room and there she told
What her lovely mistress said.
His eyebrows went up in his head
When he enquired the lady's name
And duly was then told the same.
He grabbed his cloak and said, "Lead on,
I will tell no one where we've gone!"
And so they got back to the house
And straight away she did announce
To the lady that she'd brought
Back the gentleman she'd sought.
The Lady did not show surprise
To see the wrinkles, scars and eyes.
She said "Good evening, this reception
Concerns us both in a deception.
For though you are not yet aware,
This is your second visit here!
Earlier a comely youth
Educated and quite couth,
Attempted in this room to woo
Me, while saying he was you.

Forgive me if I lack discretion
When I say your reputation
Preceded you and I'd enquired,
Should my company be required
By you, all about your looks,
Life style, even taste in books.
And so I really was surprised
To see this young man's watery eyes,
When I'd expected ones of steel.
You can imagine how I'd feel.
Now you know why you are here
Sit down my Lord, and take good cheer.
Have some wine and let us plan
How to snare this sly young man."
The Lord relaxed into his seat
And sipping at his wine took neat
Began to laugh and said "I fear
Madam, I have an idea
Which if it works will never let
This simple puppy dog forget
How he tried to deceive you.
Come, this is what we must do."
And so they planned into the night
And drank and laughed with all their might
And then they both retired to bed
And there, I think, enough is said.

But let us move on to the day
When the Squire was due to pay
Another visit when he thought
He would get what he had sought.
He knocked and duly was admitted
To the house where he submitted
To the maid his sword and hat,
After which, behind the fat
And ageing lady's maid
He went upstairs where all was laid
For a meal for only two.
"My mistress is awaiting you"
She said, and pointed to a far
Door which had been left ajar.
So she left him all alone
And then he heard a voice say "Come.
Come my Lord, have no ado,
In my bed I wait for you.
For since I saw your handsome face
I confess, I cannot wait!"
Oh, silly Squire, how he rushed in
To the room where he thought sin
Lay awaiting him in bed,
"Madam, I am here!" he said.
While under all the covers lay,
With nothing showing I should say,

The object of his great desire.
"Blow out the candles, noble sire"
He heard her voice demand of him
Which he did, and then was in
That great four-poster in the room,
Swathed in tapestries and gloom.
Then leaning over her, said "Dear,
Won't we kiss now I am here?
Pull the covers from your face
That I may know your sweet embrace."
Back the covers came and stark,
And naked in that bedroom dark,
The Squire kissed and kissed again
And then, as though he was in pain,
Let out the most almighty cry.
It was the kind that you and I
Might emit in great surprise,
The poor young Squire was horrified.
For stubble scratched his tender face
And he'd found something else in place
Of what he had expected lovers
Searched for underneath the covers.
At this point the room was filled
With light and all the curtains pulled.
The Lady stood there with her maid,
While in the bed the Squire laid

Next to a man who laughed and said
"I thought you'd prefer me instead!"
The Squire thought that he would die
Lying by his Master's side,
While the Lady laughed then sighed
And stared the young man in the eye.
"Now let this be a lesson, boy
Lest you should try a similar ploy"
She admonished him and then
The Lord said, "Squire, for your sin
I could turn you on the street
But simpletons can't earn their meat.
But learn your lesson if you can.
There are many kinds of man,
Some are lords and some are squires
And neither of them should aspire
To anything but what they are.
You're lucky that you played with fire
And did not get too badly done.
Now get dressed, and get you gone!"
It was a sorry Squire that night
Who crept home worried by his plight,
But his Master had such fun
From what the stupid boy had done
He gave the Squire a second chance
And ever since that evening's farce,

He has been a model Squire,
Doing as his Lord requires.
Not a word said out of place,
No jealous looks upon his face.
The lesson being harshly taught,
He learnt and now is greatly thought
Of by his Lord who, in a way,
Should thank the lad for such a day
As the one where unforeseen,
He met the Lady of his dream.
So now all live a happy life,
The Lady soon became his wife.

And so, my Lord, that ends my tale
Of how a silly, simple male
Was caught out, but here I'd add
Not all men are like that lad!"

The King had laughed so much his cheeks
Were stained by tears and all their streaks,
Then smiling called out "Lady Smee,
A thousand thanks from all and me
For entertaining us so well.
It is a spicy tale you tell!

And now, dear Lady, I must find
Someone else to pass our time.
All this laughing leaves me tired
And so perhaps it is desired
That now we have a tale less rude,
More moral, maybe and so who
Should I call up to recite
The third tale of this arduous night?"

Now, in the corner by the fire
Dozing sat a holy Friar,
While the light from out the grate
Reflected from his shaven pate
And danced in patterns on his face,
He seemed to sleep in holy grace.
Thin but ruddy, strong but mild,
Grown man yet still a child,
This poor Friar was singled out
By the King who, with a shout,
Woke him from his slumber fair
By kicking at his ancient chair.
"Come now Brother!" called the King,
"Wake up! Look lively, here's a thing,
To sleep with so much going on,
We want a tale, and you're the one

Who's going to keep us all amused.
Come now, don't feel so abused.
If a sinful King like me
And our ageing host, Lord Smee
Can keep awake, then so much more
Should you whom angels all adore."
The Friar was a gentle man
And smiling, said "My Lord I can.
Sitting here I did not doze,
But merely listened with eyes closed."
"Ha! this Friar has a wit"
Cried the King, "now go to it
My holy brother, tell us all
How to avoid the dreaded fall
From holy grace and to be saved
From the error Adam made."

The Friar sat up and looked around
And as the laugher all died down
He said "I think I have a tale
Complete with moral here for sale.
The price? Attentive ears and all
To listen wholly with the soul."
And having made this introduction
Settled down with this instruction.

The Friar's Tale

A monastic life is not for all
And most who join receive the call.
But others join, not grace to find,
But with more worldly things in mind.
Bread and meat and ale each day,
Modest work and naught to pay
Makes quite a change from sweat and toil
Or ploughing at unfruitful soil.
Now in a monastery south of here
In a group of brothers dear
To me, there was such a fellow
Who outwardly was pious and mellow.
When a priest was there, he'd be
Attending him or on his knees
And those in charge thought much of him.
"He does not understand a sin"
They would whisper as he passed
His hands together, tightly clasped.
When his masters were around,
He made sure he could be found
Within sight and sound of them,
And being monks, but also men

They were led to think him pious,
His fellow monks knew otherwise.
For on his own and in with them,
He was quite the worst of men.
Secret drink and women too,
Offensive quite to all those who
Reprimanded him for acts
That really took them quite aback.
He swore and criticised the place
And called them sissys to their face
And constantly got on their nerves
Until at last one monk observed
"Brothers, we have had enough!
And we are made of sterner stuff
Than tolerating ever more
The ghastly habits of this boar.
Therefore I suggest a plan
To teach to this ungodly man
That it's not robes that make a monk,
Or rosaries and all that junk,
But what goes on inside his heart
That causes him to stand apart
From sinful ways that others take
And so some plans we must now make
To either rid ourselves of him,
Or turn him from his path of sin."

All agreed and gathered round
And talked and argued 'til they found
An idea that they thought may work.
Then practising – they did not shirk –
Until they felt they had it right.
Other monks worked through the night.
Needles, cotton, shears as well
Were all concealed inside their cells.
Cloth was stolen, some dyed red,
The rest was just left white instead,
Until at last the stage was set
And once again the brothers met
To decide upon the date
When this monk should meet his fate
In an attempt to cleanse his soul,
Or rid them of him once for all.
The eve they picked duly arrived
And while the monk in question dined
Privately within his cell
Other monks busied themselves.
Two of them dressed up that night,
One in red and one in white.
One in white had wings outspread
And a halo on his head,
His face was whitened with some chalk
And he had practised how to talk

In a slightly different manner
From his usual rowdy banter.
While the other red hose wore
And a cloak and even more,
Painted bulls horns rather crude
From his temples did protrude,
And on the hose a tail was darned,
He carried it looped on his arm.
What a pair these brothers made,
Monks involved in escapades
Are very few and far between
But serious was their demean.
As the bell tolled 10 o'clock
To the cell they duly walked
And gently pushing-to the door
Walked into the cell before
The very eyes of our bad monk,
You should have seen the poor chap jump.
"As I said when we last met
This fellow deserves all he gets"
The monk in red said to the other
"Come now, not so drastic brother"
Said the monk dressed all in white
"Harsh judgments are not always right.
We were saying up on high
Just the other day, to fry

And boil in your place one must do
Things almost as bad as you.
Come now, Satan, he's your soul
And I know that all his goals
Are selfish, greedy and quite bad
But still, he's only just a lad."
"Just a lad!" came the retort,
"This monk's a really evil sort.
Saint Peter, I'm surprised at you
For sticking up for someone who
That, even now, I know can see
Will make hell his destiny.
His soul is mine, it's coloured black,
So give up now, I'll take him back
With me when I go tonight.
Come now Peter, let's not fight."
It was a startling revelation
To the monk, this conversation
Laying out his soul all bare
By the visions standing there.
He gulped and said "I do repent.
Saint Peter, don't let Satan vent
His evil vices out on me.
Help me! Give me sanctuary!"
But the two continued talking
And sedately took to walking

Round his cell and from their stare
He felt they knew not he was there.
He waved his hands and shouted loud
And soon drew to his cell a crowd
Of other monks who asked what ailed,
As he stood and quaked and quailed.
"Can't you see them here inside?
Can't you see?" the bad monk cried,
"St. Peter's here and Satan too,
Beware they do not visit you!
I am doomed, it is my end.
I do not possess a friend
In this world I thought so fine."
"Brother, you've drunk too much wine!"
Said the others, "sleep instead,
Drink some more and go to bed!"
And laughing loud they took their leave
But they were laughing up their sleeves
And still the two continued chatting
"Well," said Satan, "he's so lacking
In the stuff that monks require.
Do you really still desire
To try to mend a soul like that?"
"I do" Saint Peter answered back,
"You may be right, that I do fear.
Perhaps we should return next year

And give the fellow one last chance
And if he should refrain perchance,
Then his soul with me will dwell,
If not, then take him down to hell."
"Very well" Satan agreed,
"A year, then he belongs to me."
"We'll see" Saint Peter then replied,
"Goodbye now Satan, keep inspired!"
"You too Peter, keep you well"
Then they both walked out the cell.
All night long our poor monk sat,
All night long to dwell on that.
And in the morning on his knees
Made confession to the Priest.
To him he poured out all his sins
Asking God would forgive him.
And from that day, completely altered
That same monk has never faltered
From the straight and narrow way
And many men are heard to say
What a saintly monk he is.
His brothers love him much for his
Kindness and humility,
Grace and generosity.
And so, my Lord, here ends my tale,
I hope in it I did not fail

To teach as well as to amuse.
Do you think that you approve?"

The King replied "My thanks and more,
Your lesson cannot be ignored.
You show that wisdom can still rule
O'er the artful and the fool.
If a monk as bad as he
Can be restored to sanctity
How much more then is there hope
For we lay and simple folk.
Finally I offer you
My apology, it's due,
For striking at your chair tonight,
It must have given you a fright."
The monk looked up and gave a smile
Then whispered after a short while
"Your noble apology you keep,
I should not have been asleep!"

The King looked round and said "I see
Some of the gathered company
Are showing signs of tiredness.
Would you all prefer to rest

Or are you happy to go on?
Do speak out, for though the storm
Seems to ever gather force
Some to sleep may yet recourse."
But at his words Sir Robert Smee
Said "Stories do not tire me,
I've not enjoyed a night so much
Since when I married, and as such
I say let's have another tale
And perhaps some meat and ale!"
"Bravo good Smee!" the King replied
"With food and drink we're well supplied
And so, good ladies, it's your turn
To tell a tale that all may learn
The secrets you keep hid from men.
I'm sure there are a lot of them!"
A serving woman round and plump
Holding ale and pies looked up
"A tale your Majesty requires?"
She shouted out, "may I enquire
If a tale from me will do?"
"Madam, may I welcome you"
The King responded, "down your tasks,
Your platters and your leather flasks,
My ears are hungry for your words,
So set you off and do your worst!"

The woman laughed, as did the rest,
While under her enormous chest
She crossed her arms and then leaned back,
Her dirty clothes hung loose and slack,
Her feet were planted well apart
And in this posture then, she starts.

The Serving Woman's Tale

 A marriage is not made above
With choirs and angels, truth and love,
But mostly – for the likes of me
It's made for practicality.
It's made to keep the larder stocked,
It's made so front doors can be locked.
It's made so children shouldn't starve,
It's made so land can be worked hard.
Such a marriage I'll speak of,
It was mis-matched, there was no love.
The wife was cold, her tongue was sharp,
And he was cruel, big and dark.
Many times he beat his wife
To within an inch of life.
He was a brute, a bully too,
Never was a man so cruel.
And so they trudged through every day
Acting in unsavory ways,
Until one evening before dark,
As the wife was ending work
A stranger on a milk white steed
Came riding by, and fair was he.

A gentleman of noble bearing,
Everything that he was wearing
Spoke of taste and quality.
His eyes were kind, he had the free
And easy way that seems to shout
Of those who've never gone without.
And as she stood and stared at him,
The woman was so taken in
By his looks and fair demeanor
She did not see what lay behind her
And stepping backwards tripped and fell.
"Damn!" she cried "Oh blast" and "Hell!"
Such dainty words came flooding out
Not such a whisper, more a shout
And you would think a well-bred gent
Would be quite shocked at such a vent
Of vulgar language, but not him,
Instead, dismounting, looking grim
He said "Dear Lady, pray let me"
And helped her up on bended knee.
He brushed her down, apologised
And said "I see that I surprised
You, riding up the way I did,
I hope that you will yet forgive
Me for the distress I cause.
For as a knight I'm bound by laws

Of chivalry and I declare
I was upset to see you there."
Poor woman, all her life abused,
Now by this man so gently used,
Something that was quite her fault,
Another takes the blame for. What
A revelation, what a change.
Quickly then, her thoughts arranged
She blushed and twittered "Quite alight,
I often find this time of night,
Sights and sounds can get distorted"
At which the man duly retorted
"For your words I am right glad
And yet, good lady, I feel bad
About the harm I've caused to you"
"Pray sir, now don't make ado"
The wife replied, now in full swing,
"Do not think another thing
About this paltry incident,
Already I've forgotten it.
On your horse, be on your way,
It's now past the close of day."
So saying this she sought to clasp
The bridle of his patient horse
And handing him the reins she smiled
And waved goodbye and then retired

Into her hovel of a home.
My goodness, how her thoughts did roam,
All that night and all next day
About the courtesies he'd paid
Her and even greater than,
Was the contrast between men.
Her ugly husband, hard and rough,
Cruel and nasty, dark and gruff,
The fair young knight, all manners kind,
Lightly spoken, good in mind.
Until her mind began to plan
Upon a way to change her man,
Nothing that she did or said
Would change what went on in his head.
To magic then, she must resort
Although she was not quite the sort
Who normally believed in it,
She sought the service of a witch.
In a hut all filled with smoke,
Our stalwart wife entered and spoke
"Sister of the dark and shade,
From whom both good and ill are made,
Help me out with my problem,
How to change the way of men."
The witch looked up and laughed aloud
"Indeed, you're living on a cloud"

She cackled, "every day in life
I have a visit from a wife
Who has the same request as you,
There's little here that I can do."
But the wife was anxious now
And sitting down then told her how
Events had slowly come about
To make her feel she's all wrung out.
Patiently the witch heard all,
Then pulling up her darkened cowl
Took a piece of bone and hair
And held them high up in the air.
From her lips an eerie chant
Issued forth and then she burnt
The strands of hair upon the fire
And holding out the bone enquired
Of the wife if she'd demure
To take the gift she offered her.
"You indeed have cause to want
That which many really don't.
Your case is just, you've been ill used,
All your life you've been abused.
Take this bone, it's from a Saint
And every night upon the plate
Your husband takes his daily bread
Grate a little of this dead

And whitened bone upon his meal
And very soon he'll start to feel
A happier man, a better soul,
That life's quite pleasant after all.
He'll feel remorse and sorrow too
For the way he's treated you
And very soon your man will seem
Like the one found in a dream.
Once the bone is ground away
Its good effects, you'll find, will stay
And it's unlikely he'll revert
To his former ways, but first
Just before you leave my house,
A warning I must first espouse.
Food can come all rich and sweet
And you feel you'll never eat
Enough to satisfy your taste
And yet, you soon forget your haste.
The richness sometimes gets too much,
The sweetness claws out at your guts
And shortly then, you start to feel
The need to eat a plainer meal.
Something bitter, something tart
You find is what you want at heart.
And so be warned you too may find
That you are of the latter kind

And if you do, come back to me,
And we will see what we will see."

"On no" the wife cried, "no, not I
To have a man as you describe
Will be heaven sent, refrain
From saying I'll be back again."
And with that she paid the crone
And hastened back the road to home.
So every night from then we see
Our wife so surreptitiously
Grating bone on all he ate,
Luckily it had no taste,
And very soon a change began
To work itself upon her man.
First he started to say please,
And then his shouting all but ceased.
He helped her when he'd finished work
To clean the home and sweep the dirt.
He called her 'dear' and brought her flowers
And whiled away the evening hours
By playing with the children or
Greeting people at the door.
Very soon her work grew less
She had more time now, thanks to his

Startling change of attitude.
The trouble was, with less to do,
And all his help and saintly ways
Her patience now began to fray.
She lost her temper, got quite snappy,
Frustrated that he was so happy.
The more he did, the more she asked,
Even the most menial tasks,
Nothing that he did was right.
She even sought to start a fight
And gradually the roles reversed
Until one night she even cursed
The day she'd gone to see the witch
And took the gift that caused the switch
And rendered her the nasty one.
Reflecting then on what she'd done
She sat upon her husband's knee
And said "Please listen carefully."
She told him what she'd done and why
And how although she'd tried and tried,
With his improvement came her fall
"I have no kindness left at all!"
She cried and asked him to forgive
Her for how she'd made him live.
He took her in his arms and said
"Do not cry, have joy instead.

For since you fed me holy bones
I so enjoy my life and home
And despite your bitter hue
You know I'm still in love with you.
It seems a pity then to spoil
A squeaky wheel that just needs oil.
Go again and see the crone
And obtain another bone
And if you partake of it too
It should also affect you
And so we shall have joy as yet,
So dry your eyes and go and get
Another bone and then you'll be
As happy and content as me."

Full tilt she ran till she arrived
At the smokey door and dived
In amongst the dirt and mess.
"I saw you coming, I confess"
The witch said to her "I'm surprised
You took so long to realise
That the warning which I gave
Had some truth, do you behave
Like he was before, my dear?"
And brushing back a salty tear

The wife said "Yes, you were quite right
But I don't come to you to fight
For something that will change him back,
Rather give me what I lack.
Grant me then another bone
To make ours a happy home.
Many lessons I have learnt."
Already the old crone had burnt
The hair upon the fire and gave
The wife the present that she craved.
"Return then to your happy home,
It shall be so and now be gone."
She told the wife who left right then
And ran back to the best of men.
Living in this graceful state,
Gave thanks each Sunday to the Saints!"

"A handsome tale, and moral too,
There are hidden depths to you,
Noble wife" the King observed,
"If I had known that I was served
By a woman with such wit
I should take more note of it.
I must say that I liked your tale,
It's good and wholesome, like your ale."

✳

While all this was going on
Outside raged the evil storm.
Snow was mingling with the wind
And the cold was creeping in.
"Stoke the fires! Bring more wine!"
The King called out, "how goes the time?"
And yet it was still early hours
"Another tale we need for our
Enjoyment and our edification"
The King said, "even education.
Whose turn next to entertain
And divert us from this rain?"
All was silent in the hall,
Then a man stepped forth and called
"Your Majesty – I think you fail
To appreciate the joy of ale,
You sup your wine, but if you knew
The care it took to bring to you
The golden liquor, foaming free
Made for you by such as me,
You might deign to down your cup
And instead to fill it up
With the fruits of English beer,
Such as you may imbibe here."
"A brewer sir?" the King retorted

"I'm sure your beer is well reported.
I do not shun your drink, but wine
Is drunk in smaller cups and mine
Is not different, there's a reason,
In this cold and chilly season
Too much beer means too much pee,
And it's too cold outside for me!"
"I cannot argue with my Liege"
The brewer readily agreed
"But if I may, I'll share a tale
Of rivalry inspired by ale.
It's quite alright, the tale well ends,
The two involved both parting friends,
But my tale will serve to show
Just how low a man may go
To prove he is the very best
And a cut above the rest."
"Your tale sounds perfect" said the King
And I'm sure is just the thing
To take our minds off storm and snow,
So make a start man, off you go!"

The Brewer's Tale

A brewer of a noble court
Loved the joy his ale brought.
It was revered throughout the land
T'was said he had a master's hand.
Rich and golden, clear and fine
It compared with the finest wine.
But fame can sometimes have a price,
Can lead to unseen forms of vice
And when another came to brew
In a nearby town, and whose
Beer was different but as good
It changed our brewer's happy mood,
From gay and lively, never hurried,
To a man obsessed and worried.
Every day he'd watch for wagons
Coming by weighed down with flagons.
Every day he was mistaken
His customers had not forsaken
His fair brew for what was found
For sale within the neighbouring town.
But curiosity is fickle
And gradually a steady trickle

Of our brewer's faithful brothers
Stealthily sampled the others.
At darkness they'd walk briskly down
And drink up in the other town.
It was not long before they went
In daytime too, and gaily spent.
Our brewer watched his custom go,
The other watched his coffers grow.
It's also very sad to say
It did not work the other way
The other's brewer's faithful drinkers
(Obviously more rational thinkers)
Drank their beer and stayed at home
And did not feel the need to roam.
Our poor brewer could not stand
Not to have the upper hand
So asked a friend what he should do.
His friend advised "If I were you
I would disguise myself and try
This other beer and work out why
Your customers are leaving here
And drinking up your rival's beer."
"My rival?" thought the brewer, "how
Had I not realised this 'til now?
A rival, taking trade away,
I'll go disguised, and go today."

So dressed in cloak with hood around
He set off for the other town.
Ordered beer and supped and then
Ordered more and supped again.
It was potent and well made,
The other brewer knew his trade.
Our brewer quietly went to pay
Then closed the door and stole away
From the busy tavern thinking,
While his old customers stayed drinking.

Winter turned to Spring and then
Spring to summer once again.
The Castle Lord of both the towns
Declared "Ladies, put on your gowns,
Men dress up, I do declare
Next week we shall have a fair!
Jugglers, acrobats and clowns
Food and drink will fill both towns."
But now the Lord had to decide
From where the ale would be supplied.
He asked his nobles and his squire
Which brewer's services to hire.
Our brewer gazed at empty flasks,
As the other brewer was asked.

Sad and angry, hurt and scorned,
In his empty tavern stormed
Our injured brewer, 'til a plan
In his tortured mind began
To bring about the others fall,
He had no scruples left at all.
First he gathered stinking weeds
And handfuls of brown rotting leaves,
Collected dead rats by the score
And dirty sweepings from the floor.
Putrid mushrooms, rotten eggs,
From empty barrels mouldy dregs,
Insects, worms, a few dead frogs,
And the piss from local dogs.
In his cellar kept it there
Until the night before the fair.
Then as the towns went dark and slept,
Down the hill our brewer crept,
An open brewery window found
And quietly, without a sound,
Crept inside complete with sack
Carefully balanced on his back.
Rows of barrels stretched away
Ready for the fair next day.
On the floor his sack he slung
And pulling out each wooden bung

Dropped a handful of the slime
In each barrel in the line.
Three quarters of the barrels corrupted
The slime ran out, and interrupted
By the sound of noise outside
Decided he had better hide.
Was silent 'til the noise had gone
Then tidied up and went back home.
The next morning both the towns
In festive mood hurried around,
Setting up the stalls and tents
The tables, food, and all were bent
On making sure it was all there
And ready for the coming fair.
The brewer too set up for sale,
Thought one more time he'd check his ale.
He felt proud, the ale purveyed
Was the best he'd ever made.
He poured a jug and took a drink,
My God, you should have seen him sink
To his knees, his face turned green,
It was like nothing you have seen.
Like a madman then he ran
From barrel to barrel, jug in hand
But every one worse than before,
Until he stopped, could go no more.

Head in hands, he sobbed and prayed,
As the minutes ticked away.
Knowing when they start the fair,
There would be no ale there.
He racked his brains, then paused and frowned,
Perhaps the brewer in the town
Next door would have some ale to spare
To save the day and save the fair?
He hurried up the steps and still
Hurried faster up the hill
To the tavern of the man
Whose jealousy and wicked plan
Had brought about his current state
And engineered this dreadful fate.
"Brother Brewer, help me please!"
The man burst in and on his knees
Said "All my barrels have turned sour,
As you can see the midday hour
Is very nearly here, I pray
That you'll help and save the day?"
Now our brewer, full of glee
To seize his opportunity
Was about to say "I'll do
The ale stall then, in place of you.
I'll sell my beer, it's lucky that
I've got plenty in the vats."

Of course he had been brewing madly
Anticipating this and gladly
Thinking of his great success
As he destroyed the happiness
Of the other brewer, but now
When it came to seeing how
Distraught the man was and how sad,
Our brewer really felt so bad
He asked himself 'What have I done?
This is not like me. I've some
Nasty traits behind the bar
But now I see I've gone too far.
I've allowed my jealousy
To rule my heart and now I see
The sad results, I've been a fool,
How could I have been so cruel?"
To his credit then, he said
"Don't fear my friend, all is not dead.
Let's check all your barrels now,
I can't believe that all are sour.
Then we'll blend your ale with mine,
I'm sure the taste will be divine.
We'll take the markers off my kegs
So none will know. We'll use your pegs.
I'll help you, but none will surmise
That this is a joint enterprise."

At this the other brewer's face
Was transformed and he embraced
Our brewer and then off they went
To check the barrels weren't all spent.
Of course we know a full one quarter
Were still full of goodly porter.
Our brewer loaded up and carted
Down his barrels and they started
To mix the ales and all was done
As the fair was just begun.
The ale sold well. "Now here's a thing
This beer is fit to serve a King!"
The Lord pronounced, "you must show
Your brother brewer how to go
About creating such a brew
So he can make as good as you!"
Our brewer winced but did not say
What had taken place that day
But the other brewer cried
"No, my Lord! No, it is I
Who needs the lessons, I declare
That my goodly brother there
Helped me out" but then he paused
As the other brewer caused
Him to cease and look his way
"What my brother's trying to say"

Our brewer interrupted, "was
We worked together here because
The townspeople so liked the stuff
There may not have been enough.
So we combined our skills and beer
And made the ale you're drinking here."
"Well done!' the Lord declared "I'd call
You an example to us all."
And so the day was a success
And even more, I will confess
The brewers got along so well
They partnered up and now they sell
An ale brewed by them both together.
Their breweries joined, I can't say whether
Our brewer eventually did say
What really happened on that day.
Suffice to say they remained friends
Our brewer making full amends
For his act of jealously.
So let him an example be
To those of us jealous of others,
Be they strangers, friends or brothers,
Be kind and careful what you do
Lest it be done instead to you!

The King looked round and said 'I fear
There is not one assembled here
Who has not one time or the other
Felt jealousy about another.
You told it well, I like the way
The brewer's conscience won the day.
Morals are good, like plough and harrow
They keep us on the straight and narrow.
But now I think it's fair to say
Enough morals for one day.
We need a tale of ribaldry,
Of things that everyone might see
In other people and their ways,
Tell me now, what do you say?"
"I agree" a woman bowed
Stepping forward from the crowd,
"If your Majesty requires
A tale of others strange desires
I may have just the one to tell.
It has no moral." "Just as well!"
The King declared, "it sounds ideal.
Just the sort of tale I feel
Will stir us from this lassitude
An inspire our gratitude.
Stoke the fires! Bring more light,
Get the embers burning bright.

Settle down and listen well
To what this lady has to tell.
But first pray make your introduction
Or shall I, with some royal deduction
Divine your role? It is my guess
You are the castle laundress."
"My Leige is clever" she replied
"How was I then identified?"
"Easy Madam" laughed the King
"Your sore, red hands are just the thing
To keep the doublet and hose
Smelling sweeter than the rose.
Without your help we would all stink!
Undesirable, I think.
So if you would, please tell your story
And if it is a little bawdy
So much the better I would say,
I doubt we will be lead astray
By what we are about to hear,
Now off you go, I am all ears."

The Laundress's Tale

Washing clothes is unforgiving
If undertaken for a living.
But there are many who must scrub
With hands in water in the tub.
And while, as work, its hard and tough
And makes your skin and hands go rough
It also gives some indications
Of other peoples' inclinations.
Clothing is a second skin
That all of us must wear, and in
The choosing of it give away
Something of ourselves. It says
A lot about our taste and thus
How the world should regard us.
But underneath the drapery
Are things that others do not see.
Licey vests and pants unclean,
You'd be amazed at what I've seen.
Like a canker in a rose,
The outside may deceive the nose
But delve within and you will find
A perfume of a different kind!

But fear not, my story's theme
Is not about what is not clean
But more to do with secret places,
Disguised identities and faces,
How what we think we hear and see
May not be what they seem to be.

So, to a court a young man came
He was fair and not the same
As most of the uncomely youth
Who usually were quite uncouth.
Manners he had by the score
And took great pride in what he wore.
Softly spoken, slightly shy,
He served the lord and did not try
To join the games and nasty brawls
That often took place in the hall.
But when it came to swordsmanship
None could beat him, on his hip
He wore a sword inlaid with gold,
It came from Persia, so I'm told.
Light as a feather in his grasp
You've never seen a blade so fast.
He moved so quick he seemed to prance,
He made a fight seem more a dance.

As he leapt, he'd point his toes,
They looked right fair in purple hose.
His legs were shapley, long and slim.
As you can tell, I fancied him!
Unfortunately, as you'll see
He never ever fancied me.
Although he was a boy of charm
And many a maid longed for his arm
I never saw him court or woo
Which was surprising for one who
Had so many charms to fete,
That is until the Lady Kate
Took up residence and then
You should have seen the castle men
Stare in disbelief, aver
They'd never seen the likes of her.
Six foot two or maybe three
She'd stand there towering over me,
Arms with sinew, muscle too,
Long black hair and eyes of blue,
A grasp that nearly crushed your hand,
She didn't wear a wedding band.
Softly spoken, watchful eye
She'd sit and watch the men go by.
I do believe they were afraid
Of this tall and doughty maid

Except that is, for our young man
Who seemed besotted rather than
Intimidated by our Kate.
Every morning he would wait
And escort her through the hall,
Dine beside her, shunning all
Who dared to perhaps criticise
This woman of enormous size.
I watched them both most carefully,
If you have a job like me
You learn to speculate, inspired
By how your customer's attired.
A fancy coat may seek to hide
A tattered doublet worn inside,
While those with just the plainest hose
May have quite different underclothes!
I wondered then what secrets lay
Beneath our lovers' overlay.
I must confess I had suspicions
But as a woman of discretion
Did not voice them, but instead,
Just kept them quietly in my head.
Until one day the young man asked
If I could wash for him and passed
A bundle to me, plus my fee
And left, but now what do I see?

Apart then from the purple hose,
The doublet and the well-made clothes
Tucked inside, perhaps forgot,
His underclothes. I felt quite hot
As I unravelled them to clean,
But they were not what I had dreamed.
Instead of linen or fine wool
They were of silk, I felt a fool
As I stood gazing at the stitching,
So finely done, it was bewitching.
You must imagine, if you can,
What I then felt about this man,
And as for Kate, what would she feel
If ever then he should reveal
What was usually hid away,
I really would not like to say.
I kept my counsel, washed and cleaned,
Gave them back, but also schemed
To tuck them back into the hose
So by the time he knows I know
It is too late for him speak
Best just pray that I'm discrete,
Which of course I am, you know
We washerwomen have our code!
He and Kate, like two young doves,
Continued then their courtly love

Until a knight arrived requesting
Hospitality, suggesting
In return for bed and board
He'd enter service of the Lord.
It was agreed, the knight could stay,
But very soon all rued the day.
His faults were many, he was vile,
A bully, bigot, full of bile
Envious of all and more.
His name, Sir Edwin de la Torre.
Now when he saw our young man fight
Besting all the castle knights
In their daily practising,
He stepped into the combat ring.
Said 'I do not like what I see.
I think it's time you fought with me!'
He looked around and cursed and spat,
But did not see Kate where she sat
Every day to watch the fighting
In her young man so delighting.
Now I saw her fix her gaze
On Sir Edwin as he raised
His sword on high in an attack
On our young man, while his back
Was turned, you should have heard the gasps.
But our boy was very fast

And turning, parried Edwin's blade
And swiftly then his Persian-made
Sword sliced the air and cut the hand
Of the other slower man.
Sir Edwin roared and slashed and hacked
The fast young man fought bravely back
While all the time, our Kate looked on
Her face was grim, all pleasure gone.
Sir Edwin's sword swung down, he laughed
And broke the Persian blade in half!
He struck again, a blow to tell,
The young man stumbled back and fell.
Sir Edwin raised his sword on high,
But at that moment came a cry.
He looked around, eyes full of hate
Coming face to face – with Kate!
In her hand she held a blade,
I swear that it was blacksmith made,
Four foot long and made of steel
It would have made a giant reel.
She swung it high like it weighed naught
Engaged Sir Edwin and they fought.
She beat him back with every blow,
Round the ring I watched them go.
He chopped and stabbed but could not win
Kate had the better then of him.

Until the young man called her name
She turned and Edwin's last chance came.
Striking out, his aim was rotten,
He split her bodice top to bottom.
Then Sir Edwin just stood there,
All that he could do was stare,
For through the bodice came not breasts
But a broad and hairy chest!
Rippling muscles, lean and tough
Kate was made of sterner stuff
Than her clothing had belied,
And disguised what lay inside.
The young man called out once again
And hearing him then call her name
She smiled at Edwin, softly said
'Goodnight' and hit him on the head.
I should add she used the flat,
Not the blade edge to do that,
Although it would have served him right
If Kate had put out all his lights.
Over to her love she ran
And kneeling down said "I'm a man.
I suppose that now you see,
You'll not feel any love for me?"
Just dazed, our young man smiled and sighed
And said "I too have a surprise,

For though I may appear a man,
I am a maid, it is a sham."
They gazed into each other's eyes
And both together realised,
Man and maid belong together
It doesn't really matter whether
One is dressed up like the other,
If love is true for one another.
So happily they settled down,
She with her sword, he in his gown.
Real love conquers all, it's true
And here ends my tale for you.
I hope that it has entertained,
Kept you happy and sustained?"

The laundress looked up at the King
Who pointed, and said "Here's a thing.
My good woman, what can I say?
This is the best tale yet! I'd pay
A ransom to have seen the face
Of Sir Edwin when Kate chased
Him round the ring. I'm glad she served
A blow to him he much deserved.
Outward trappings can deceive,
A pretty girdle, coloured sleeve

Can take our eye, and in that part
Blind us to a person's heart.
Man or maid, if love is true,
It really doesn't matter who
Wears the trousers or the dress,
It's love that counts, forget the rest.
So now, what next? Smee! You decide
Where our next tale may yet hide.
You've entertained us, fed us well,
Perhaps you've got a tale to tell?
I'd be honoured, noble knight
If you would share a story, might
You have a tale of far-flung places?
Different languages and faces?
Exotic cultures, foreign ways,
Tell me now, what do you say?"
Sir Robert Smee then, bowing low,
Said 'My Lord, I can't say no.
A tale I have, if please you Sire
From lands so hot, they burn like fire.
Where camels roam and scorpion
Scuttle in the noon day sun."
"Excellent!' the King declared,
"Someone, get Lord Smee a chair.
Sit down my knight, and take your time
Good stories are much like good wine,

Consumed slowly, greatly savoured,
Relishing their many flavours.
For kindness that you've shown us here
In my heart I hold you dear.
Nobility's a state of mind
It's open-handed, courteous, kind
And I must say of all those who
Are noble, none more so than you.
And so I'm sure your tale will be
Of valour, generosity."
Sir Robert Smee sat down and blushed
As round the hall the chatter hushed,
He took a breath and cleared his throat
Then all went silent as he spoke.

Sir Robert Smee's Tale

Life is precious, as you find
When in a battle, left behind
You turn to face a giant foe
Intent on killing as they go.
Their sword is poised, make no ado
Their next victim will be you.
And so you duck and turn and fight
And beat them off with all your might
And if you're lucky and they're tired,
All their energy expired
You seize your moment, take a breath
And despatch them on to death.
It is a grim way to survive,
To ensure you stay alive
And sometimes I still feel remorse
For those I've fought with in the course
Of my long and hard career,
I'm glad to now be resting here.
Most battles last less than a day
At least that's usually the way
But once, as a much younger man
Fighting out in foreign lands

I fought in one that lasted two,
Hard to believe I know, but true.
We started once the morn was light
By our Lady, what a fight.
There were two thousand of us strong
The other side had less. A long
Line of soldiers waiting ready
For the word, we all held steady
Till the trumpet sounded, then
We galloped heading straight for them.
Some were mounted, on foot some
We thought the day already won
As the lines met, sure were we
By night of gaining victory.
How wrong we were, how very vain,
To think numbers alone can gain
The upper hand. For it is skill
That enables men to kill.
Their archers like no other then,
Felled a full one hundred men
Before we even reached the line
And still they simply they took their time.
Then deadly sharp, we met their lance
Our horses did not stand a chance.
The Knights unseated, they were down
Their horses struggling on the ground.

And now the enemy assayed
Killed the knights there as they laid.
We all engaged, the fight was on
Their warriors were skilled and some
Fought not with one sword but with two,
My Lord, I do not jest with you.
Scimitars flashed through the air,
With a short sword also there
To despatch the careless knight
Who dodged the blade but lost the fight.
As we approached the end of day
Some five hundred bodies lay.
Most were ours, I broken-hearted,
Many friends were now departed.
Regrouping then we nursed our sorrow,
Prepared to fight again tomorrow.
Fighting there was not for me
I much prefer home territory.
With rocks and boulders, dunes and sand
It took a different kind of man
To fight continuously in the heat
Not submitting to defeat.
We thought we'd have the upper hand
In that bleak forbidding land,
Our numbers made us doubly strong
We thought we'd win, but we were wrong.

By daylight then, the fight resumed
Now by the need to win consumed
We fought hard back on the rebound
We pushed them hard and gained some ground.
Into the midst, I strove to win
Hacking, slashing limb from limb.
Steel whirled above my head
While all around me lay more dead.
Then from the tumult came a figure
Dressed in silvered armour, vigour
Seemed to spring from every part
Of this warrior, and my heart
Missed a beat as I could see
The man destined to defeat me.
On his brow a golden band
Marked him out a different man.
He was a King, I had no doubt
His manner, bearing, seemed to shout
Of noble blood, and in this strife
I knew this man would take my life.
We stood apart and faced each other
Warrior brother to warrior brother.
I swear he bowed before he raised
His sword, sun glinting on the blade
Then we engaged, the fight begun
Beneath the unrelenting sun.

He beat me back with such a skill
In my dreams I see him still,
His dark eyes staring into mine
From his dark face, seeming to shine
As he advanced, and I defended
Knowing how the story ended.
'Til suddenly he was distracted,
Glanced away, and I reacted
Swung my sword down on this man
And knocked the scimitar from his hand.
Surprised he stood and stared at me,
Then smiled and knelt down on one knee
Head held high, he made a bow
And waited for the final blow.
There was no sign in him of fear
I only saw a great man here.
A man of true nobility
Kneeling now in front of me.
I knew that if I struck the blow
The enemy would turn and go.
No army fights without its King
We'd be the victors, but something
Deep within me stayed my hand
Instead I reached out to him and
Beckoned him back on his feet,
I did not wish then to defeat

An unarmed man, 'twas not my way
I said 'Shalom' and walked away.
We fought on in that awful heat
Until, afraid that we'd be beat
The order came to just pull out
So gradually we turned about
And backing off then from the fight,
Many of us just took flight.
I was bringing up the rear
Still fighting as the time grew near
To make escape and save my breath
When I came face to face with death.
From the grave pursuing hoard
Came a man so tall and broad
I swear he was some six foot ten,
An awesome warrior among men.
He strode towards me, bent on killing
But my poor body now unwilling
To carry on, gave in and failed
I raised my sword to no avail.
Staggering back under his blow
I hit the ground and watched my foe
Raise his weapon, smile at me,
As I embraced eternity.
As the sword came down I prayed,
With my maker peace I made,

Crossed myself and felt no shame,
But the ending never came.
Another sabre then I see
To stop the one destined for me
Placed in its path, knocked it away
As I just watched from where I lay.
The big man turned to face his King,
Bowed his head, said not a thing
But stepped aside lowering his blade
While on the sandy soil I laid.
The King extended me his hand
And grasping mine, helped me to stand.
He took my arm, looked in my eyes
And then I truly realised
Here was a man above them all,
With true nobility of soul.
He walked with me, his men made way
To where the edge of battle lay
Then bowed and bade me carry on,
Raised his hand and said 'Shalom'.
I joined my men and then we left,
Far fewer now, we were bereft
Of friends and brothers, uncles, fathers,
I tell you now that I much rather
Fight on England's green terrain,
Than in those desert lands again.

We boarded ship and sailed for home
I've stayed here ever since, I roam
Not much further now than Kent,
A pleasant place when last I went.
But when the sun shines and it's hot
Memories I think forgot
Come flooding back and still I see
The dark eyes of the King on me,
I feel his hand, I see his face
In that distant desert place.
We both live now thanks to the other,
My enemy and yet my brother."

Finishing his tale Lord Smee
Before the King stood silently.
The King looked thoughtful, rather grave
And said "More knights as you I crave.
How easy then to kill the King
And yet you did a nobler thing.
To spare a life of one unarmed
To step back, let them go unharmed
Lies at the heart of chivalry.
I wish then such nobility
Ran through the blood of all of us,
Put to the test, would we all pass?

Would we all do as then you did
Our inner cruelty kept well hid?
Or to our basest urges yield
Kill with no mercy on the field?
And let us not forget that he
Repaid your generosity
With equal measure, spared your life
Escorting you out through the strife.
This King, you do not give his name,
Puts many other Kings to shame.
I fear I could not safely say
I'd do as he did on that day.
I hope I would. And now I think
You must sit down before you sink
Onto your knees, my good Lord Smee
Accept these heartfelt thanks from me.
Your tale was great and it was true,
I truly do admire you.
And now what next? It's hard to say
Where good tales in this midst may lay?"
The sound of bells then filled the air
And yet it seemed no one was there.
"What was that? Who made that sound?"
The King asked quickly glancing round.
"Twas I" a voice said from behind,
"Twas I. I thought you would not mind."

Then into view came such a fellow,
Dressed in brightest blue and yellow,
Bells adorned his shoes, his head
Encased in a strange hat of red,
A pointed face and bright blue eyes,
He leapt up, to the King's surprise
And landed neatly by his feet.
"My King, my Liege, pray let me greet
My noble Sovereign", then he bowed,
Laid down, rolled over, laughed out loud,
Leapt up before the startled King
Dancing then began to sing
"If an answer you can't find
If problems vex your troubled mind,
Look in a book, go ask a Priest,
Seek your friend's advice at least.
Rack your brains, but if they fail
Your thinking then to no avail,
If the wise cannot help you
There's only one thing left to do.
Do the opposite of the rule,
Don't ask the wise man, ask the Fool."
The King leant forward, said "Come nearer
So that I may see you clearer,
You move so fast, it's hard to see.
Don't be shy, come up to me."

The Jester took two steps then stopped,
Jumped and skipped, and quickly hopped,
Somersaulted in a ring
And then sat down beside the King.
Leaning over said "I fear
You may object if I sit here?"
"Not at all" the King said smiling
"I find your antics most beguiling.
But there is a price you see,
If you remain sat next to me.
A tale is then required from you
To entertain us all and who
Better than a jester then,
Who sees the foolishness in men."
"Agreed" the Jester said while lounging
In the chair, some ale scrounging
From a passing maid. "I'll tell
A tale I think will suit us well.
My tale is for your Majesty.
You sit here with such gravity
But beneath that Kingly skin
Another no doubt lives within.
Are you happy? Are you sad?
Saint or sinner? Good or bad?
Only you can truly tell
What makes you run your kingdom well.

Look in mirrors, who looks back?
What does your reflection lack?
If the glass won't satisfy
Or is not pleasing to your eye
There's only one place left to find
Reflections of the inner mind,
To see the shape of things to come
A man needs just look at his sons.

The Jester's Tale

And so my tale is of a King
Who had four sons, a wondrous thing.
One was handsome, one was brave,
Another was just money's slave.
All these three then sought to rule,
The fourth considered just a fool.
When his brothers turned to fight
He would disappear from sight.
He had a limp and withered arm,
Sweet natured, quite averse to harm,
While they hunted he would shield
Creatures hiding in the fields.
When at court he'd seldom speak.
All his brothers thought him weak.
It was not helped that words he uttered
Lost their meaning as he stuttered.
Now, this King was growing older
Found his burdens hard to shoulder.
Feared his sons would tire of waiting,
And their feelings turn to hating
The very man who gave them life.
This King anticipated strife.

So in an effort to evade
The problems his succession made,
He called his three bold sons together,
The fourth was not invited, whether
Deliberately or just ignored,
It's hard to say, but at the door
As the others met the King
So the fool hid, listening.
The King announced 'twas time to choose
Who should step into his shoes
"But all my sons are great" he cried
"Impossible then to decide.
And so I now propose a test
To see who rules a kingdom best.
In my countries are three lands
Which I will place into your hands.
Each of you one land to rule.
I will provide you with some tools,
Advisers, knights, and sheriffs too,
Serfs and men to work for you.
Your task, to govern like a King
To show that to your land you bring
Justice, peace, prosperity,
These are what I hope to see.
After three years then have gone
You must account for what you've done.

Dependent then on all these things,
I will make one of you the King."
From a chest he took three maps
Held them out and said "Perhaps
Fairest that you each choose one,
A fair land each for three fair sons."
Each son chose, unrolled the paper
By Our Lady! What a caper!
Straight away an argument,
What land then for which son meant.
How the eldest thought the others
Had the better land. These brothers
Argued hotly, did not hear
The fourth son who had now appeared.
His broken speech not clearly heard
He closed his eyes, uttered the word
"Father!"' for the first time then
Without impediment. The men
Stopped their fighting, stood amazed
While their brother held their gaze.
Then turning to the King he bowed
Cleared his throat and spoke out loud.
"You grant my brothers kingdoms three,
Is there not one then for me?
Do you think me such a fool
That I am not seen fit to rule?

Excluded from your plans for them,
Discarded in the plans of men?"
His brothers laughed and pointing, cried
"Idiots must be denied,
There's nothing to concern you here
Best that you just disappear."
But the father raised his hand
Said "All my sons should have some land.
Forgive me, my excluding you
Was an unjust thing to do.
What's for one must be for all
Or not be ventured on at all.
I will place into your hands
Another portion of my lands.
The best has gone, it's all that left,
Of fertile soil it is bereft,
Its people poor, its income small
But better that, than none at all."
"Thank you Father" said the son,
"I'm grateful for what you have done.
I will tend this land with care."
"Listen to him standing there!"
Said the brothers, "what a fool.
To think that he could even rule
A henhouse! He is just a clown
To think that he could wear a crown!"

"Enough!" the King cried, "time will tell.
And now my sons, I wish you well.
Rule your lands in your own fashion,
But justice, mercy and compassion
Will recommend you much to those
Whose care within your hands repose."
All four brothers took their lands
And government into their hands.
The first, the brave one, straightway ordered
To seize the lands along his borders.
Immediately went to war
Anxious to acquire more.
But wars cost money as he found,
His policies were far from sound.
The money quickly disappeared
And by the end of the first year
He retrenched, began again,
It was a poor start to his reign.
Neglectful of his peoples needs
They suffered and the land grew weeds
Where once was corn and pastures green
Now just wilderness was seen.
The second brother, you'll recall
Was fair and handsome, broad and tall,
He loved fine clothes, he loved attention,
But most of all, his own reflection.

"A King must have a crown" he said
"To sit upon his noble head.
I am a King, in all but name,
I think that I should do the same."
He took the taxes, called the jeweller
Said 'Make a crown fit for a ruler."
He spent the money on himself
Leaving nothing on the shelf
To run the country, build the barns,
Store the crops, maintain the farms,
Help the needy and the poor,
Instead this brother just took more.
He built a palace, failed to see
That all around was poverty.
His ministers despaired and railed
Against him, but to no avail.
And so, to brother number three,
Who only loved his Treasury.
From the first day that he started
There was no prospect he'd be parted
From the gold that filled the chest,
This brother, he loved money best.
When urgent matters needed doing
Or serious disputes were brewing
His first thought always was the cost,
Considering what might be lost

Instead of what the gain may be
In terms of love and loyalty.
He scrutinised the peasant tax,
Said 'A King must not be lax',
Ordered that his men take more
From those who were already poor.
As to the rich, he readily
Extracted their wealth steadily.
A fee for signing writs and deeds,
A price for arbitration needs,
Legacies, inheritance
Were subject to his ordinance.
No one then escaped his greed
He had no regard to need
Except his own which, simply told,
Consisted of amassing gold.
What of the fourth? the stammering fool
Who no one thought could ever rule.
On the first day he set out
Alone, and quietly walked about,
Observing, watching, taking in
The daily lives of those within
The lands which now were in his care.
He visited the village squares,
Hovels, manor houses, farms
Walking everywhere unarmed.

Talking little, listening much,
This brother had the common touch.
He chose a house of middling size,
Assembled landlords by his side
And introduced himself to them.
Awkward then amongst these men,
Stammering, explained his plan.
They listened quietly, then began
To see what he had to impart
Came directly from the heart.
What he said to them made sense
"Never mind his countenance"
They muttered, "though his speech be broken,
Better words were never spoken."
Inspired then, they acquiesced
To comply with his requests
And quickly saw their suffering land
Start to improve under his hand.
Within six months the fields were tilled
Within a year the barns all filled,
When two had passed the trade was good
Not one household lacking food.
Men were working, women weaving,
Now young men instead of leaving
Put their hands to worthwhile toil,
Turning wood or tending soil.

At the butts the archers trained,
Blacksmiths hammered once again.
Stock was raised with care and sold
And filled the coffers up with gold,
Only to be re-invested
By the brother, interested
Only in his people's care,
Happiness and how they fared.
And so the three years quickly passed,
The day of judgement came at last
To see which brother had ruled best.
They met the King at his behest
And joined him as he toured around,
Through countryside and busy towns.
To all four lands he duly went,
Inspected, questioned, this King meant
To ascertain which of his sons
Was fit to rule as he had done.
It is not hard perhaps to guess
Whose government was deemed the best.
The other three could not believe
What the fool had thus achieved.
Fool no more, a wise man then
But also wise concerning men.
He knew his brothers now would see
Him not as friend but enemy.

And so in turn he told each brother,
"It is my wish we help each other.
Help me as I rule the land
We should do this hand in hand.
While I may be King in name,
I feel there is far more to gain
If each of you took on a role,
For many parts make up a whole."
To the warrior brother then
He said "your skill is leading men,
Take the army, train them well,
Under you the ranks will swell."
To the miser, he gave more,
Said "I make you Chancellor.
With your careful eye and hand
We shall have a prosperous land."
Finally, after much thought
He made the vain one head of court,
Said "keep good manners, tasteful dress,
Chivalry, noble largesse."
And so, under his watchful eye
The others brothers satisfied,
The kingdom flourished happily,
In wealth and peace and harmony.
The old King now, his work all done,
Called to his side his clever son

And said "my boy, I'm proud of you,
I see myself in what you do.
I could not be more satisfied."
So saying that, the old King died.
There is little more to tell,
The kingdom settled, all did well,
The brothers never wrangling
Thanks to the King's skilled handling.
From idiot boy to clever King,
To judge a man's a dangerous thing.
Instead of judging you'd best rather
Look to the son to see the father."

The hall was silent, no one stirred
Neither wind nor rain was heard,
Awaiting anxiously to see
How the tale would be received.
The King looked grave, he scratched his beard,
The Jester now a touch afeared
Rose from his chair and gave a bow
Stood on his hands and enquired 'How
Did your Majesty like my tale?
Did it make you quake and quail?
Or did it tell of things and show
All that you already know?

If I displease you, strike me dead!
Imprison me, hack off my head!
Or do I please you? Give you cause
To give to me your royal applause?
Tell me all, don't keep me waiting
I cannot stand anticipating
Whether I shall live or die.
What is your verdict? Don't be shy!"
The King stood up and raised his hands
"How clever to divide the lands"
He nodded, as the Jester paled,
"You need fear not, I liked your tale.
And it applies not just to Kings
But to many other things.
Appearances deceive us all
Despite our efforts not to fall
Underneath the spell of them,
We must look carefully at men
To see the good that lies within
Hidden underneath the skin.
Your tale was good, so do not fear
You'll live to tell more tales here!"
With that the King began to clap,
The Jester sat down in his lap,
Kissed his head, fell on the floor
Rolled over, kissed the King once more

Then danced his way around the hall,
Shut the door and left them all.
The King looked over at Lord Smee,
"Thank God he doesn't work for me!"
He exclaimed "he wears me out
With all that mad leaping about."
Within the hall now there was talking,
Serving maids were up and walking
Round the people offering ale.
"What about another tale?"
Called the Squire, "it's nearly day
But there's time enough I'd say
To have one more, and here's the thing,
I say it should come from the King!"
"Aye! it should!" came the call
From all the company in the hall,
"A King's tale is what we require."
"And what about my mutinous Squire?"
Laughed the King who smiled and rose,
"A tale you'll have, but I propose
The next must come from you, my lad!"
The Squire nodded, "I'll be glad
To tell one, and with no ado,
But first of all, a tale from you!"
"You have some courage, I'll agree
To stand your ground on this with me"

The King replied, now looking stern,
"I fear you still have much to learn.
But you serve me well and more,
And so your cheek I will ignore
Just this once, so let me say,
You may have it your own way."
"God save the King!" the Squire cried
Now feeling rather weak inside
Lest he had gone too far, relieved
His comments had not been received
Badly by the King. He bowed,
Turning to the waiting crowd
Cried "Silence! We shall listen pray,
To what His Majesty will say."
The King stood up and looked around
Moved his chair and then sat down
Said "Can you hear me?" to the crowd,
"Aye your Majesty, good and loud!"
Came the answer from the hall.
"Good. A tale then, for you all."

The King's Tale

There are many kinds of men,
I think I have met most of them.
Some are faithful, some are cruel,
Some are kind, some long to rule.
We need them all, it seems to me,
To make up our society.
But in amongst them there are some
Who dwell in darker places, none
Can quite divine what fills their minds
And occupies their life and time.
They move in shadows, watching, waiting,
Masters of anticipating
What a man may say or do
Turning that to their own use.
They trade in doubt, they deal in lies,
Most are simply known as spies.
You find them in all walks of life,
Watching, cheating, causing strife.
Some sent as an instrument
Of a foreign government.
Others grown on home land
Furthering their master's hand.

The spy this tale concerns was old,
Experienced and very bold.
He'd worked for servants and for Kings
And had the skill experience brings
To judge a person by their face
And engineer their fall from grace.
His terms were simple, pay his fee
And satisfaction guaranteed.
But a spy can make mistakes
Engrossed in all the risks he takes
And find that he becomes the one
Who is being spied upon!
My tale is of two merchants then,
Two powerful and wealthy men.
The richest – arrogant and grand,
Was said to have a golden hand.
Whatever he did turned to gold.
Confident, and very bold
He flourished saying 'Look at me'
And so he made an enemy
Of the other merchant and
This other was a clever man.
Good looking, shrewd, exceeding wealthy
And by nature, very stealthy,
To the merchant's face he smiled
The other, then by him beguiled,

Called him "friend", declared "you know
We are alike, but even so
While you're wealthy, you must see
You'll never be as rich as me.
My fiscal skills beyond compare
Are something I will never share."
"Oh yes you will" the other thought,
"There's nothing that cannot be bought.
You think you are so clever. Beware.
For there are cleverer men out there!"
He hired a spy and told him "Go,
Find out what this merchant knows
That makes him what I too should be
And bring his secrets back to me."
The spy he'd chosen knew his trade,
Few were the mistakes he'd made.
Greying hair and cold blue eyes,
Stocky but of medium size,
He understood what was required
And what his paymaster desired.
His tools – experience and age
Enabled him to easily gauge
How best to gain the information,
And conclude his assignation.
But unbeknown to spy and master
The other merchant's heart beat faster

With a similar desire,
He too then, was a man on fire.
But it was not the other's gold
Or property, or lands all told
That elicited this feeling,
It was something more revealing.
His peevish wife was very plain,
Bad tempered, prone then to complain,
Cold and feckless, hard, unyielding,
Generally devoid of feeling,
Argumentative, perverse,
The other's wife was the reverse.
Young and pretty, very charming
And, what's even more alarming,
Faithful to her husband who
Took her for granted, like men do.
How his rival longed to try
The one thing money could not buy.
In short, his passions all were rife
To dally with the other's wife.
And so he also hired a spy,
Said "While such methods I decry
Go and note down what you see
And bring her secrets back to me,
For if I am to steal her heart
And persuade her she should part

From her husband, I must know
What to say and how to sow
The seeds of doubt, so she will see
The man to comfort her is me."
The spy he chose was far more youthful,
Tall and fair and, to be truthful,
Did not have the expertise
The older spy possessed with ease.
This younger spy then gave much thought
To securing what was sought,
Until at last he realised
The answer lay in a disguise.
Into his hands he rubbed some dirt,
Attired himself in tattered shirt,
And with a hat to shade his face
Looked like a man whose only place
Was cutting grass and tending flowers,
Working in some leafy bower.
Disguised then as a gardener he
Obtained work for a modest fee
At the house the man was from
Who he was set to spy upon.
Meanwhile, the older spy deployed
In the wealthy man's employ
Posing as a clerk, soon learnt
How the merchant made and earnt

The vast amounts of money he
Kept locked up in his treasury.
Every week he'd make report
To his master, even brought
Careful notes showing amounts
Recorded in the man's accounts,
Revealing how his business ran
And made him such a wealthy man.
The gardener likewise did the same
But his was a more dangerous game.
The lady often took the air
While our boy was working there,
And gradually they got to talking
While the wife continued walking.
He would show her pretty blooms,
And talk of flowers and garden rooms,
Recite some poetry or verse
Pertaining to the bees and birds,
And won her confidence 'til she
Began to talk quite intimately.
Told him how she loved her hounds,
How in her house good wine abounds,
How she preferred to dress in blue
And all the things she longed to do.
He learnt about her family,
The instruments she liked to play,

Her love of books, dislike of sport,
And put it all in his report.

The older spy meanwhile conveyed
The details for which he was paid.
Every week reporting more,
He'd knock upon his master's door
Impart his knowledge, take some wine
Occasionally he'd stay and dine.
One day, the window open wide,
The conversation from inside
Could be heard quite easily
By those in the vicinity,
Especially if – and here's the thing –
They were beneath it gardening!
And so our gardener listened well
To what the old spy had to tell
And quickly grasped the fact that he
Was talking about currency.
Money touches every heart,
There's few that choose to stand apart
From all life's pleasures that unfold
When made possible by gold.
He also quickly realised
The visitor must be a spy,

Reporting back the things he'd learnt
In return for monies earnt.
When the spy left, so did he,
Intent on following to see
Where he came from but alack,
He lost the trail and wandered back.
The next week then, he tried once more
To track the old spy to his door,
Determined now to learn the source
And subject of the spy's discourse.
This time he enjoyed more success
Discovering the spy's address
But what he saw seemed a disaster,
The spy was spying on his master!
What to do – sound the alarm?
Protect his employer from harm,
Reveal the spy who hid within
The approbation all for him?
And yet he hesitated, why?
Reluctant to reveal the spy,
To do his duty as he should,
Exposing his dark brotherhood.
Instead, he turned and walked away
Deliberating what to say,
While in the background of his mind
A plan was forming of the kind

Which, although it may seem shocking,
Was nothing short of double-crossing.
The next week dressed in cloak and hose
And not his daytime gardening clothes
He visited his master, sought
To deliver his report
While closely watching out to see
The spy who worked so deviously.
His master, then quite in the dark
Introduced him to his clerk,
Who clearly did not recognise
A brother from the world of spies.
So having bowed and wished good day,
The spying clerk hastened away
While our boy divulged his news
Of the lady's tastes and views,
And what his master needs must say
To steal the other's wife away.
She was charming, bright and fair
And as the spy sat talking there
He thought about the kind of man
That would hire a spy and plan
To steal another's money or
To steal his wife, how wanting more
For some men was their sole desire.
Then in his mind arose a fire

That smouldered as he planned and schemed
Of things he had before just dreamed.
A plan to outshine any other
To benefit him – and a brother.
Some things are better done in pairs
Like marriage, fighting, but to share
A task together you must find
A partner of a similar mind.
Our spy knew just where he could go
For such a partner, and now so
In an alleyway he waited
Hiding, with his breath full bated
Watching for his master's clerk
To make his way home in the dark.
Sure enough, the clerk appeared
And stopped to pee so did not hear
Our spy, who feeling ever bolder
Put a hand upon his shoulder.
You should have seen the other freeze
And buckle slightly at the knees
Then slowly turn around, still pissing
Only narrowly just missing
The other, obscured by the night
Who said "By God Sir! Don't take fright.
I don't intend to do you harm.
Have your pee, don't take alarm

But when relieved, I need your ear
For a short while when you shall hear
Something that may profit you
As well as me" and so these two
Once introduced, went to an inn
Where the young spy shared with him
The essence of a plan which he
Listened to incredulously.
Each spy gazed into the eyes
Of the other, for as spies
Trust is something seldom shared
And never given without care.
But united by the plan
Invented by the younger man
They both declared a common aim
Spurred on by the thought of gain,
Each then sworn to secrecy
Preserving their identity.
The old spy next day went to work,
The younger too, to tend the dirt.
By close of day the first possessed
The keys to all his master's chests.
The other also was well pleased
With what he'd managed to achieve
For though he also needed gold
Something else had touched his soul

Affecting then his very life.
He too desired his master's wife!
And thanks to all his honeyed words
And time spent talking bees and birds
And all those walks and pretty flowers
As they whiled away the hours
While her husband worked away,
In her heart the spy held sway.
She did as he anticipated,
He found his love reciprocated.
Both spies that night delivered notes
Carefully worded, nearly wrote
Purporting to come from each merchant
To the other, both marked urgent
Suggesting that the two men meet
At an inn to drink and eat
And discuss a plan which offered
To further fill their bulging coffers.
Both agreed immediately
Curious and keen to see
What the other had to say.
They locked their doors and made their way
To the inn, quite unaware
That deception took them there.
Meanwhile, the clerk unlocked the door
And gold and silver, jewels and more

Were loaded into chest and sack
Both spies departing out the back.
At the other merchant's house
They stole his money and his spouse,
And riding up behind her lover,
The three departed under cover
Of the dark, while at the inn
The merchants sat confused within,
Only to return to home
To find both wife and money gone.
The spies then went their separate ways
And never worked again, their days
Were peaceful, quiet, full of leisure
Spent in the pursuit of pleasure.
The merchants never told a soul
They'd been deceived and lost their all,
Which in the end was no surprise
For those who choose to employ spies.
And so beware of jealousy,
Of pride and greed and vanity,
Be careful what you say and do,
Lest a spy doth spy on you!"

The King sat back, no word was spoken,
The silence in the hall unbroken,

Until from nowhere came a sound
As rolling, tumbling, with a bound,
The Jester sprung up, cried "My Leige
You leave me quivering at the knees.
Is there a spy here? Let me see?
Ha! the only spy is me!
What do I spy? I'll tell you true
I spy a mighty King, that's you!
King of hearts and King of all,
King of tales told in this hall.
I am the judge and jury too,
The best tale here was told … by you!"
"Aye it was!" the noise erupted
The earlier silence interrupted
As all the gathered company
All declared unanimously
"The tale was gripping, every word.
Those merchants got what they deserved!
God Save the King! We all agree!"
The noise went on until Lord Smee
Held up a hand, demanded quiet
Before it turned into a riot.
Then turning to the King, he bowed
And said "My Lord, if I'm allowed
I too declare your tale was best,
Although I must add all the rest

Have kept us entertained full well.
But now, my King, I've come to tell
You and your court the day has come
And chased the storm away. It's gone,
The sky is brightening with the day."
"And so, good Smee, we must away"
The King replied with heavy heart
"I am truly grieved to part
From this place, yourself and all
Gathered here within the hall.
As for my tale? I disagree!
The best tale was not told by me.
A crown may sit upon my head
But it does not make what I said
Necessarily the best.
And what's more, I think the rest
Who haven't spoken may aspire
To tell a tale, and there's my Squire!
Who owes us all the story he
Should have told instead of me!
And so, dear Smee, I seek to ask
When, on our return we pass
Your castle, do you think we might
Stay with you another night?"
Before Sir Robert could reply
Within the hall a mighty cry

Went up from the company
"Come again Your Majesty!
Make it soon and don't delay!"
"There's nothing more I need to say"
Lord Smee replied, "they say it all.
My castle, grounds, food, wine and hall
Will stand awaiting your return,
Day or night the fires burn
To welcome you throughout the year
I'm honoured that my King stays here."
And kneeling down, the old knight bowed
And copying him, all the crowd
Also knelt, watched by the King
Who nodded, and then beckoning
All to stand, said 'My dear Smee
Accept these sincere thanks from me.
For I cannot remember when
I spent a better night, the men
And women who have told their tales
While we were safe from storm and gales
Have entertained us all full well.
I thank you all and wish to tell
That Squire of mine that when we next
Meet again, I shall be vexed
If his is not the first tale told
When we return here from the cold!

And now, my friends, it is adieu
I must take my leave from you
But I look forward much to when
We shall all meet here again
And comforted with food and ale,
We shall all enjoy more tales!"
"Unlock the windows! Open doors!
Unblock the gaps sealed in the floors!
Here comes the King!" the Jester cried
And led the company outside,
Where horses champed and pages scurried
Courtiers around them hurried
Mounted up the Knights sat ready
The grooms holding the horses steady.
The King, now on his noble steed
Held out his hand to Robert Smee
And said "Goodbye, my knight, my friend,
Until we shall meet up again."
His horse moved on towards the gate
Where anxious now not to be late
The gateman stood, the doors full wide,
Still scratching at his poor backside,
Bowing as they all went out,
Now anxious to avoid a clout
He ducked down low, only to find
He got clouted from behind!

The castle watched the final few
Completely disappear from view,
Then all returned to daily chores,
Washing dishes, cleaning floors,
Lady and Sir Robert Smee
Checking to make sure and see
That all was ready and made good
With stores of wine and ale and food
Laid in, not just in case the weather
Should turn bad again, but ever
Watching out both day and night
Anxious not to miss the sight
Of the King and courtiers when
They should all return again,
To talk and sup and drink some ale

And fill the hall with more lost tales.

And with special thanks to K & P